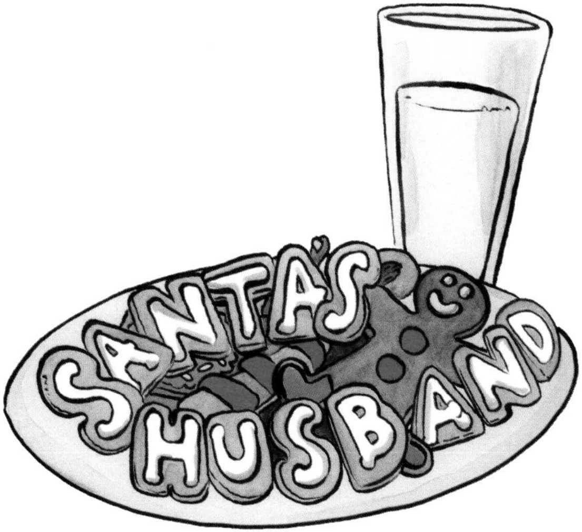
SANTA'S
HUSBAND

SANTA'S HUSBAND

Copyright © 2017 by Daniel Kibblesmith.

HarperCollins books may be purchased for educational, business, or sales promotional use.
For information please email the Special Markets Department at SPsales@harpercollins.com.

Published in 2017 by
Harper Design
An Imprint of HarperCollins*Publishers*
195 Broadway
New York, NY 10007
Tel: (212) 207-7000
Fax: (855) 746-6023
harperdesign@harpercollins.com
www.hc.com

Distributed throughout the world by
HarperCollins*Publishers*
195 Broadway
New York, NY 10007

ISBN 978-0-06-274874-4

Library of Congress Control Number: 2017938956

Illustrations by AP Quatch
Book design by Lynne Yeamans

First Printing, 2017

SANTA'S HUSBAND

BY DANIEL KIBBLESMITH   **ILLUSTRATIONS BY AP QUACH**

HARPER
DESIGN

An Imprint of HarperCollinsPublishers

This is Santa Claus.

This is Santa Claus's husband, Mr. Claus.

They are married.

Santa and his husband
live together at the North Pole,

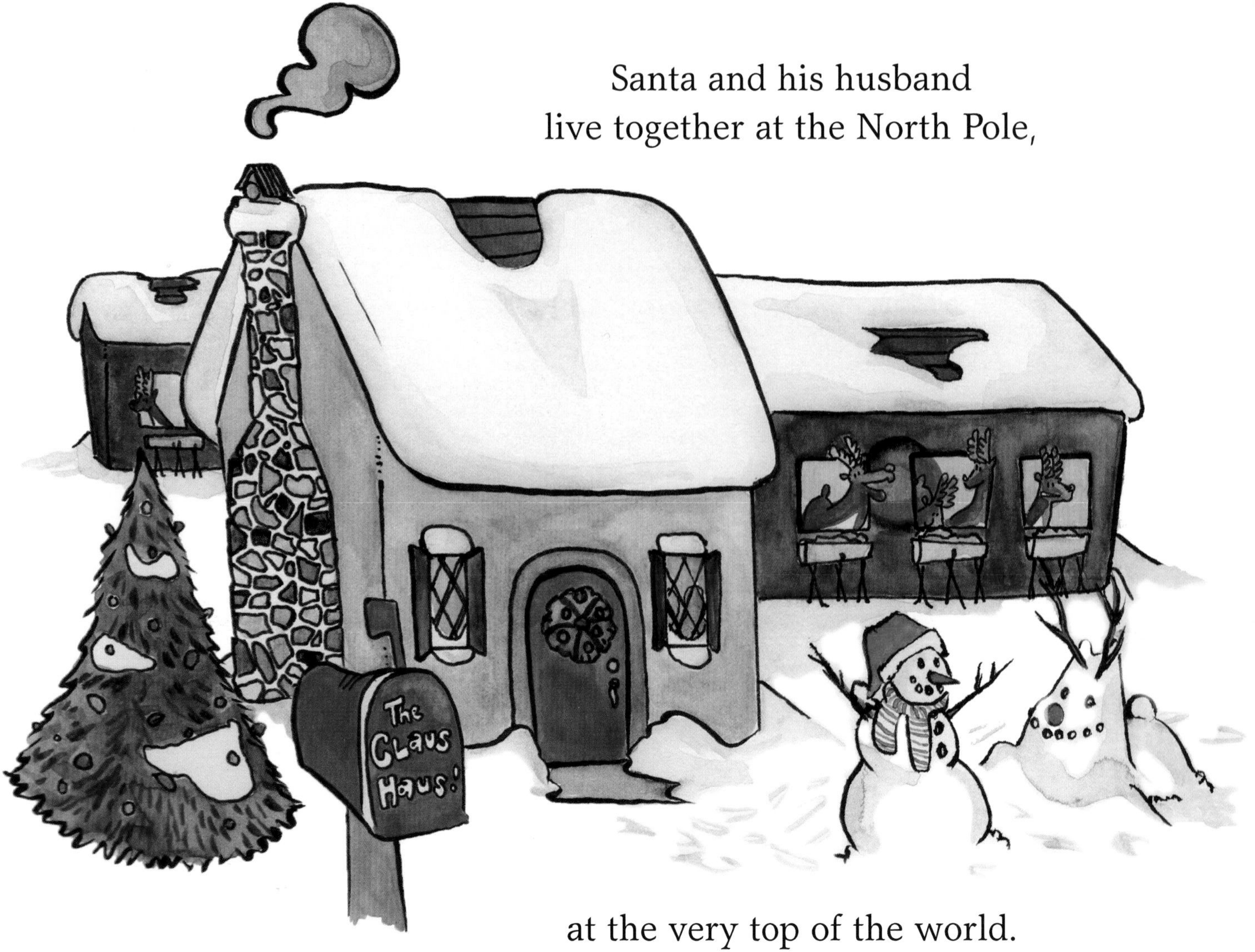
The
Claus
Haus!

at the very top of the world.

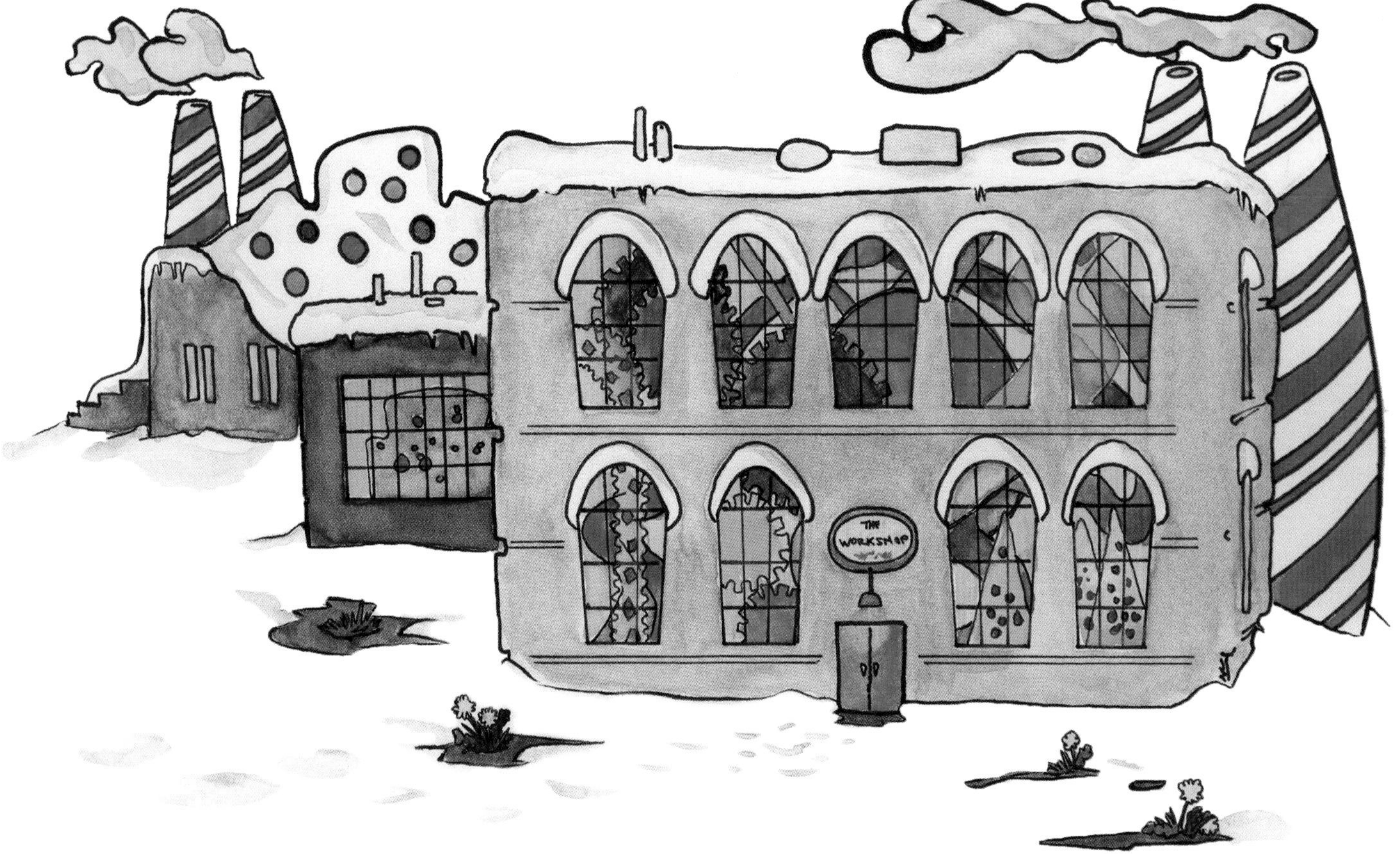
THE
WORKSHOP

They love keeping each other cozy in the cold,
but each year it seems to get a little warmer!

Santa's husband helps
Santa with all the
hard work that makes
Christmas happen.

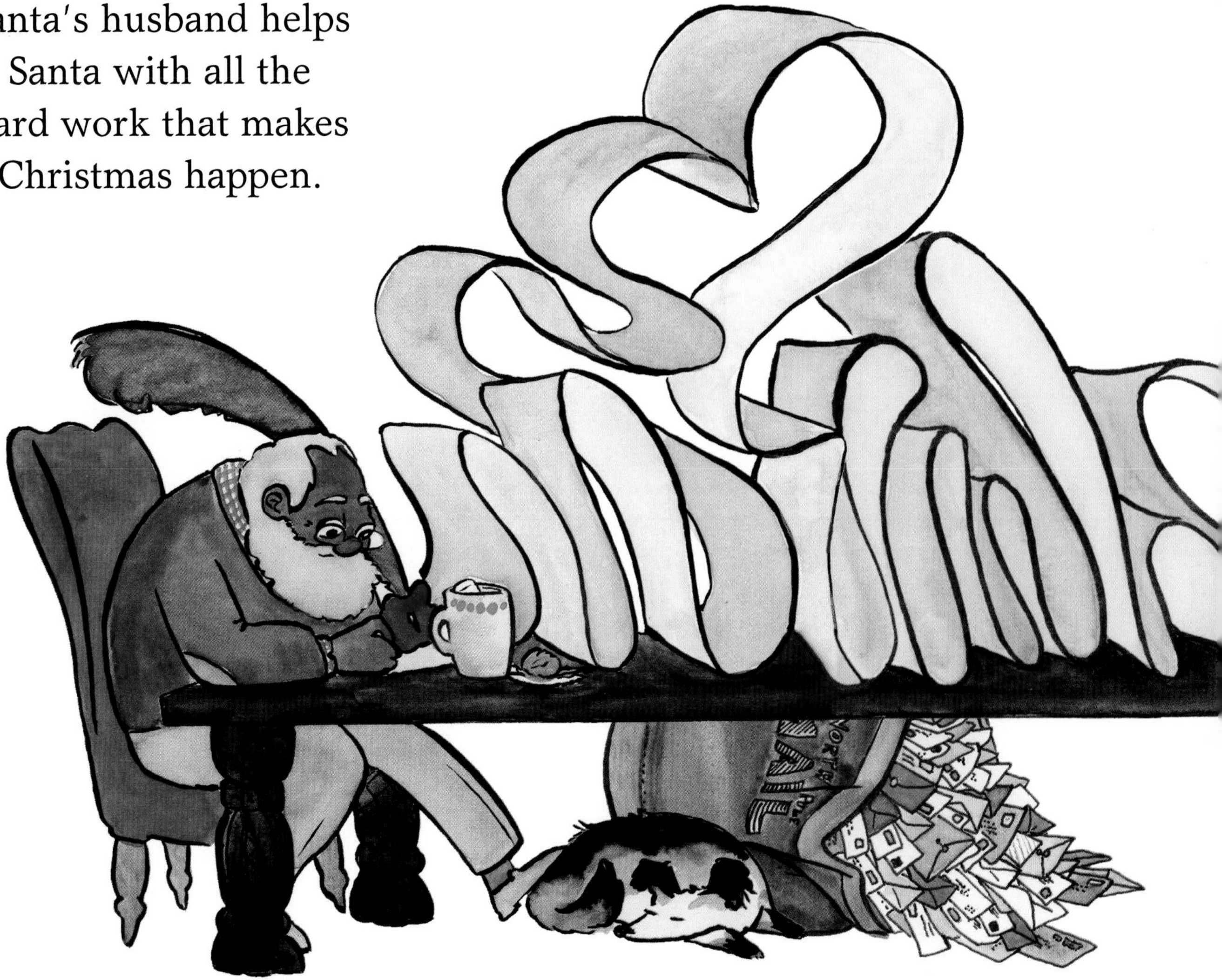

From making a list
and checking it twice...

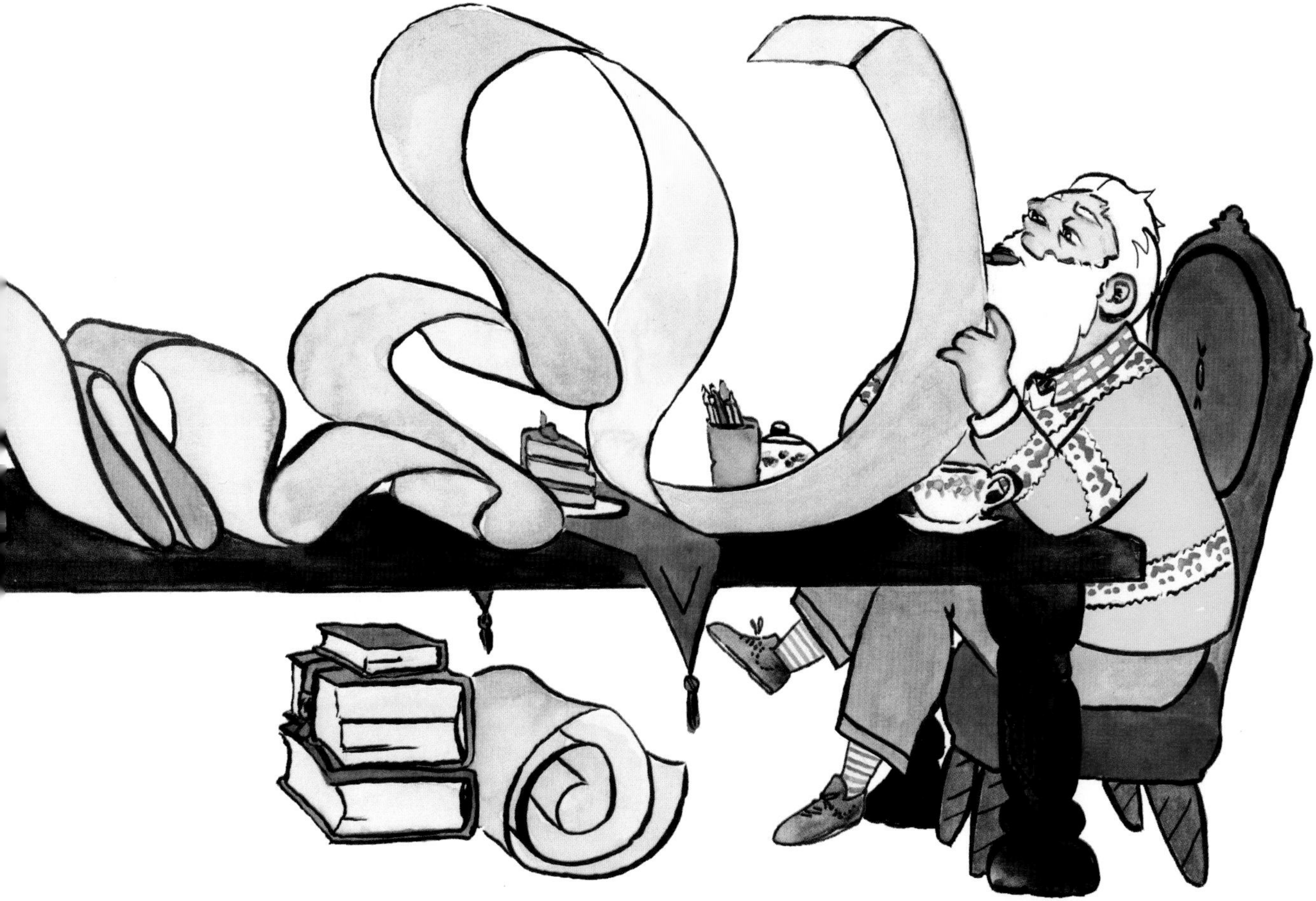

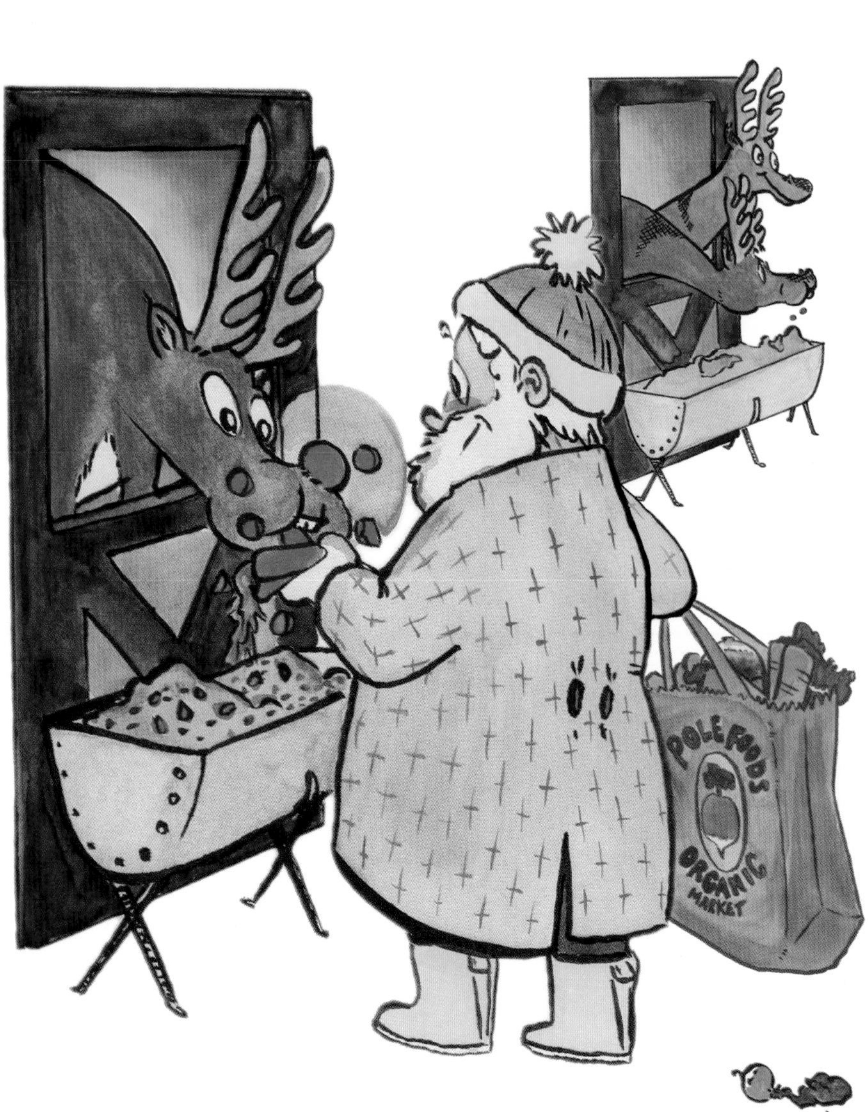
POLE FOODS
ORGANIC
MARKET

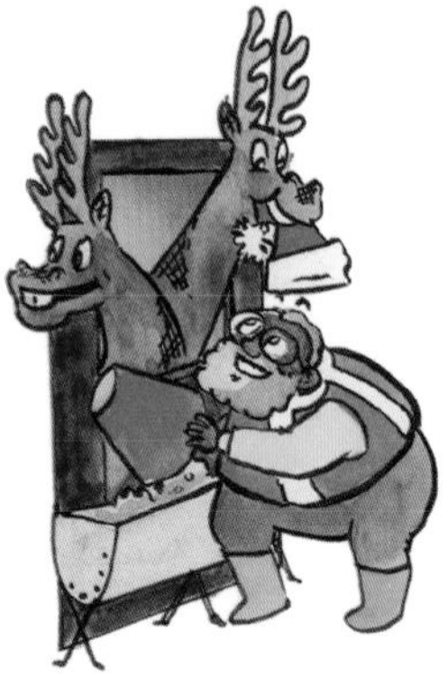

to feeding Santa's
eight tiny reindeer—
plus Rudolph, who
has special dietary
restrictions to keep his
nose shiny and bright,

to helping Santa negotiate labor disputes
with the elves in his workshop.

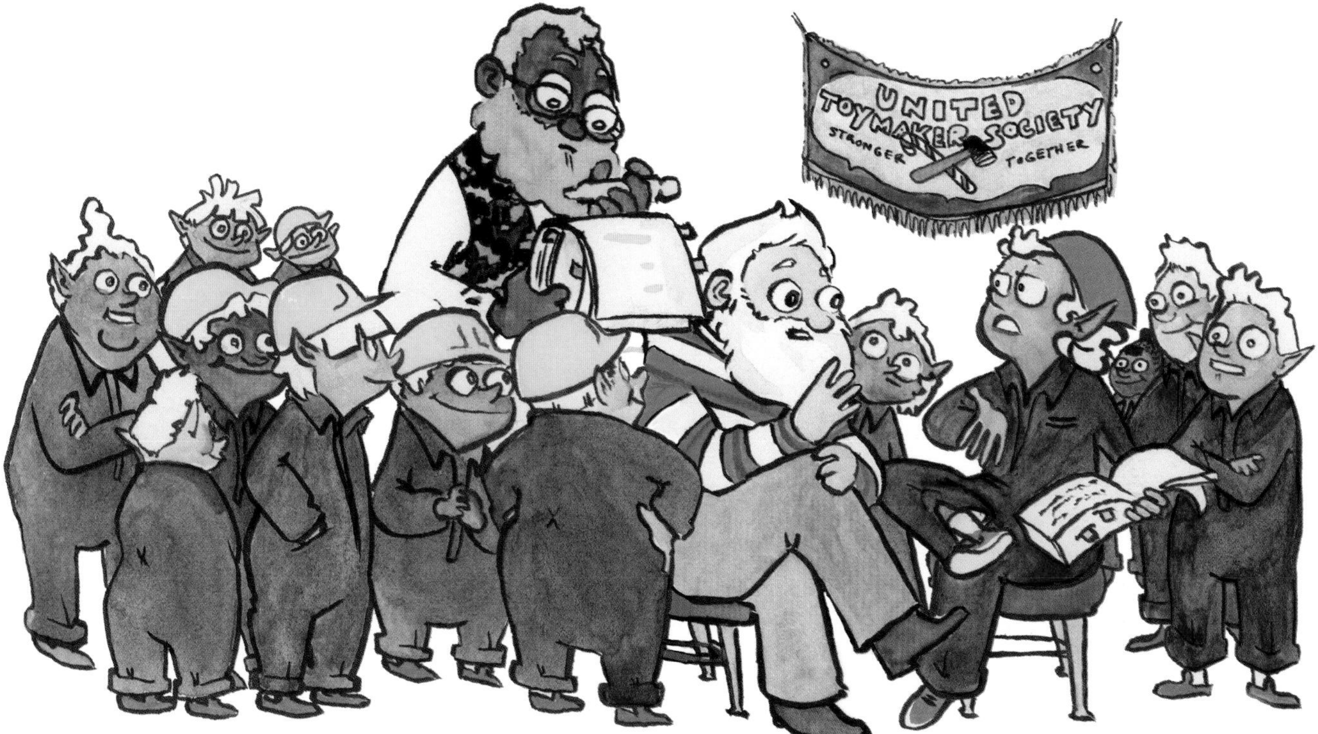
UNITED
TOYMAKER SOCIETY
STRONGER
TOGETHER

They have a spectacular dental plan.

Santa is so busy
during Christmastime
that sometimes
his husband, Mr. Claus,
even helps him out...

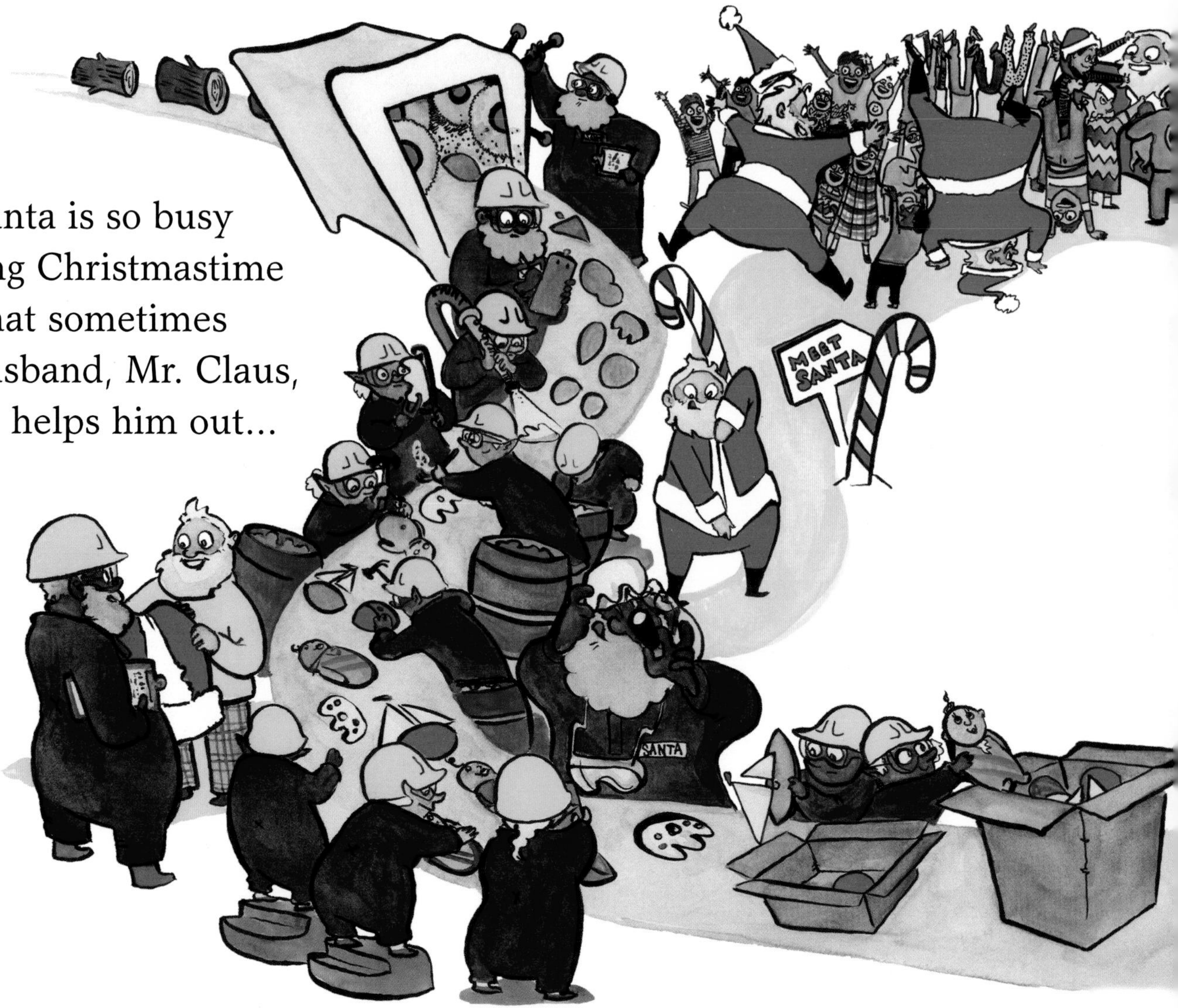
MEET SANTA
SANTA

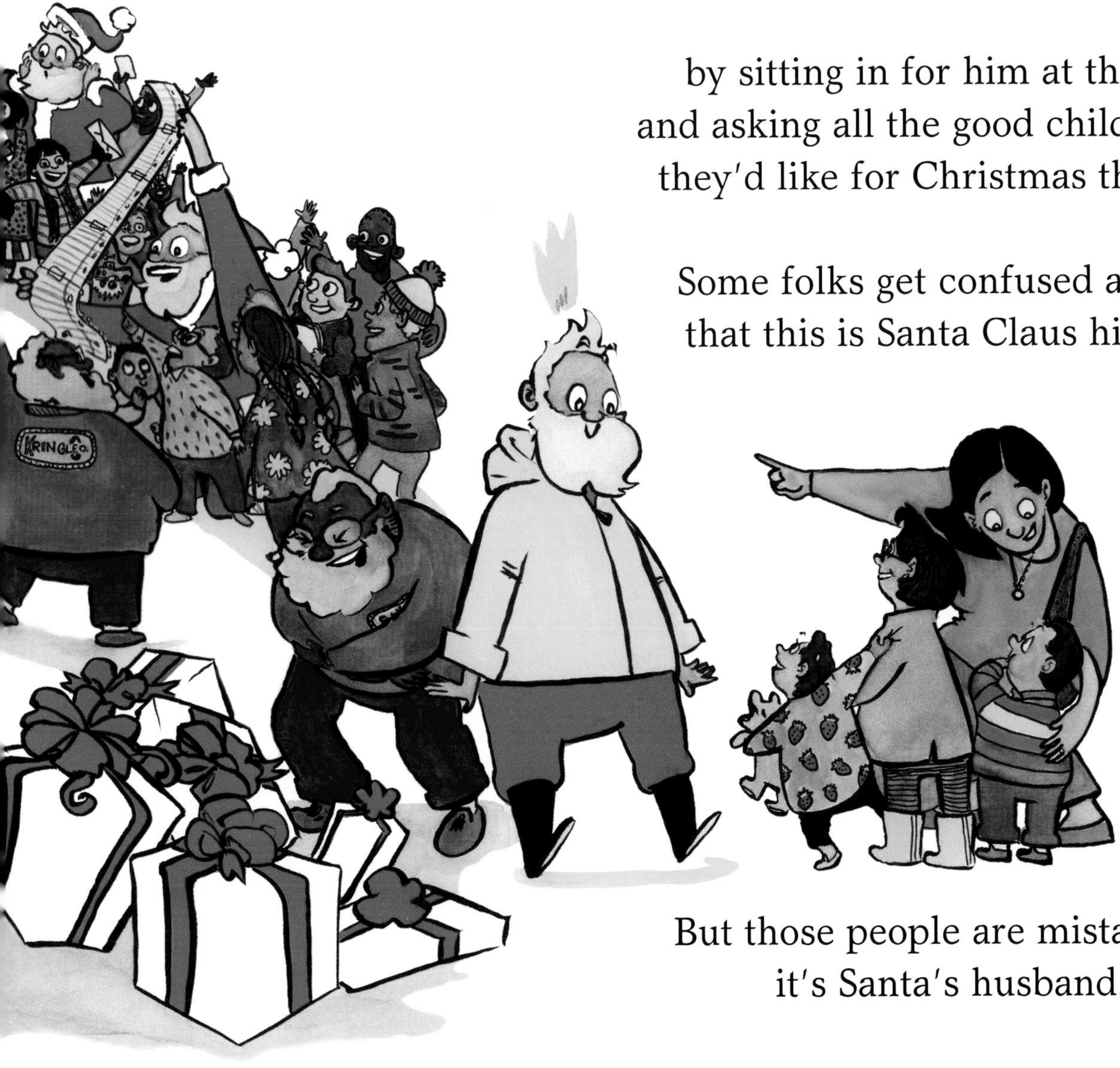

by sitting in for him at the mall
and asking all the good children what
they'd like for Christmas this year.

Some folks get confused and say
that this is Santa Claus himself!

But those people are mistaken—
it's Santa's husband.

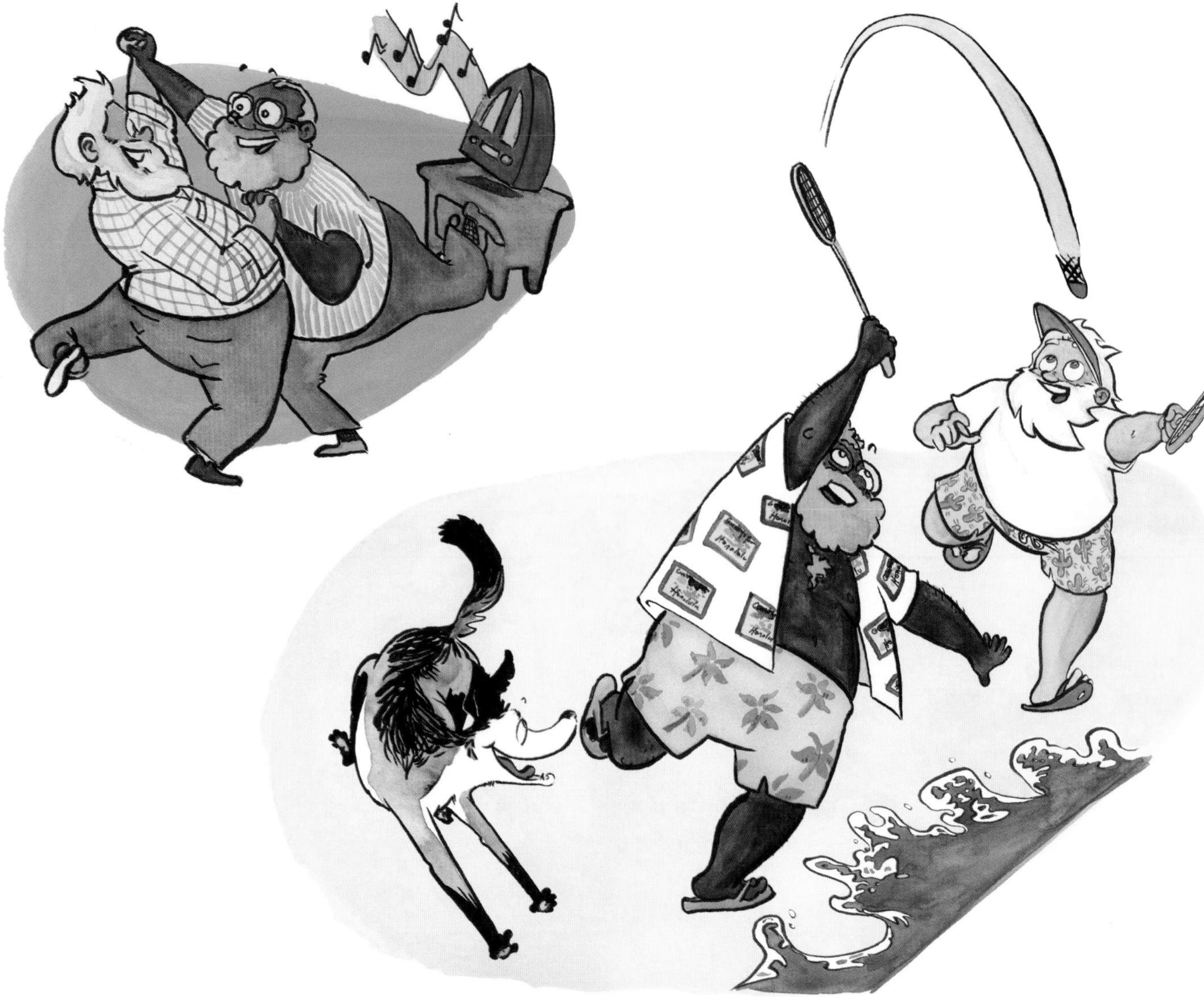

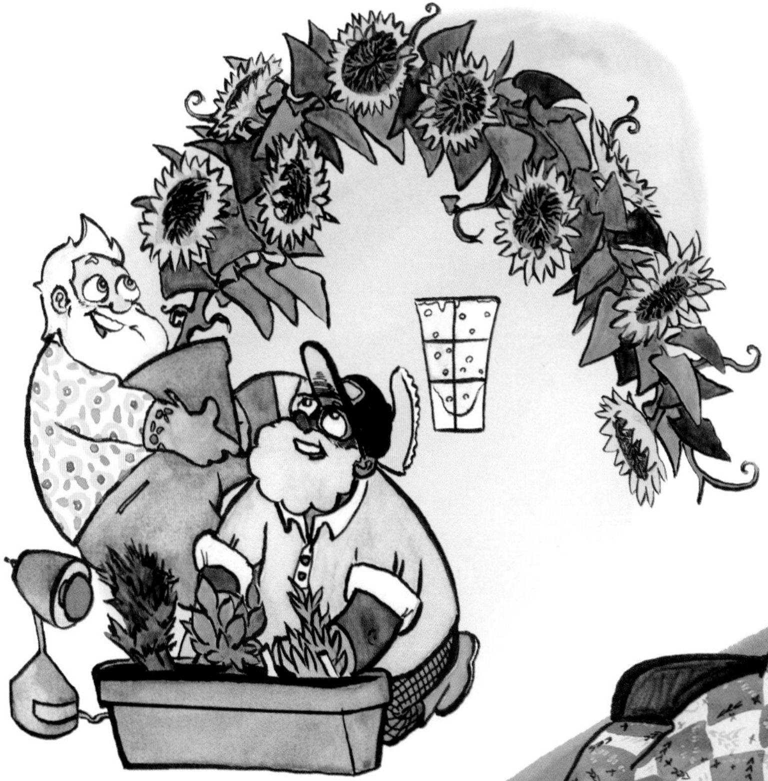

Santa and his husband
have been married in their
hearts for a long time,

but it wasn't yet official.

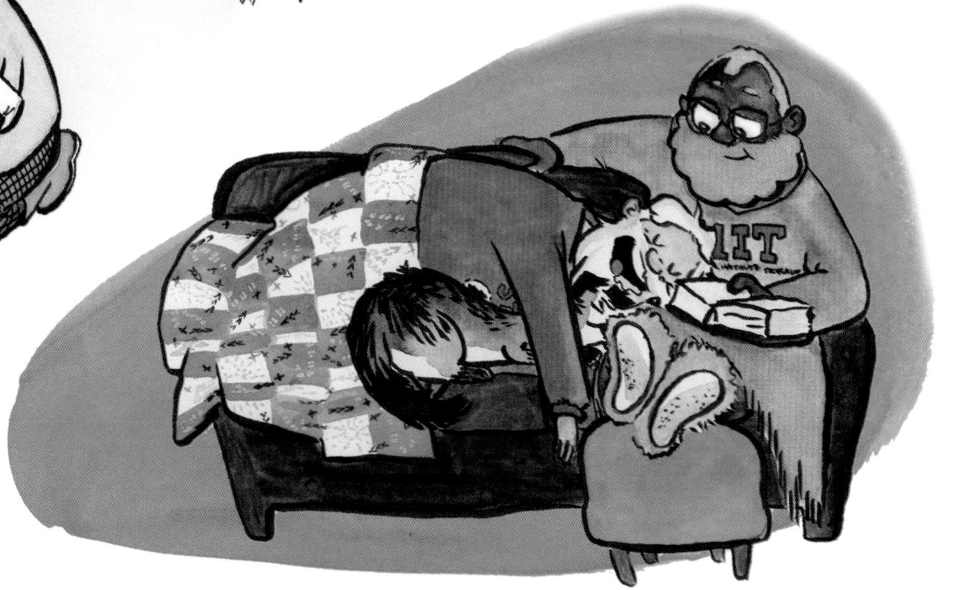
IIT

So it was a big
day when they finally
"tied the knot"!

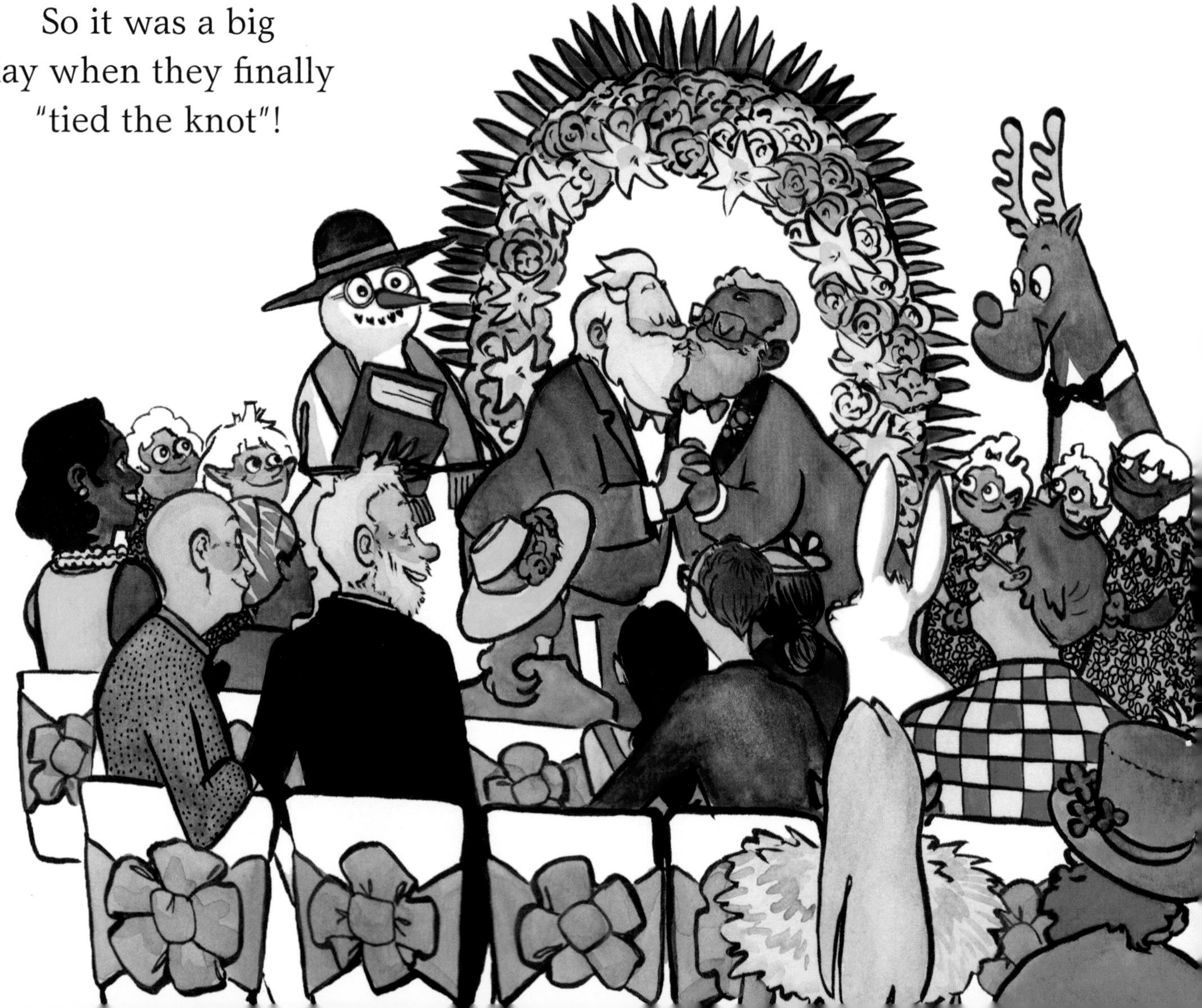

Everyone was there, from Rudolph and Frosty to Parson Brown.

Even a few celebrities showed up!

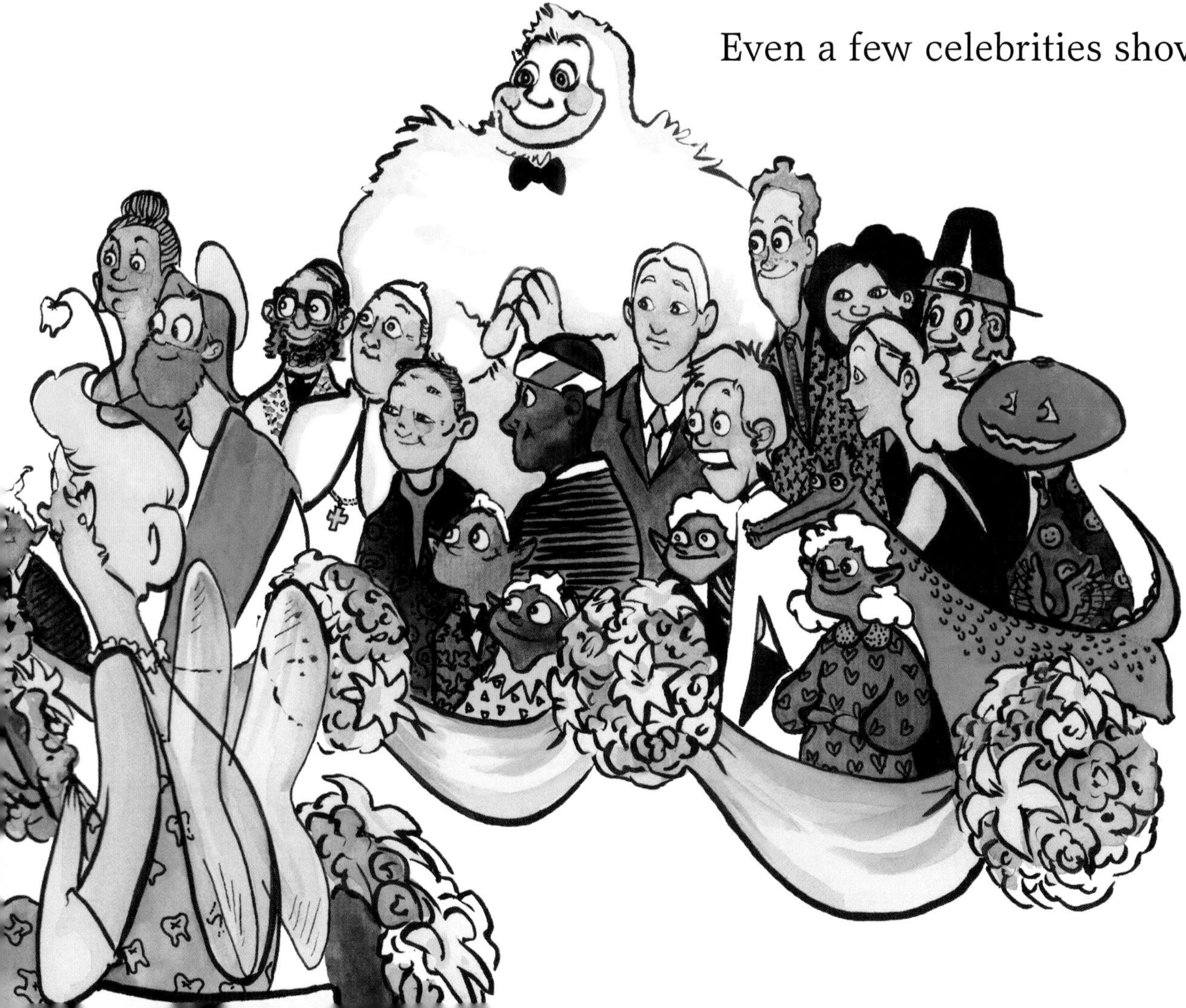

Like any married couple, they have their disagreements.

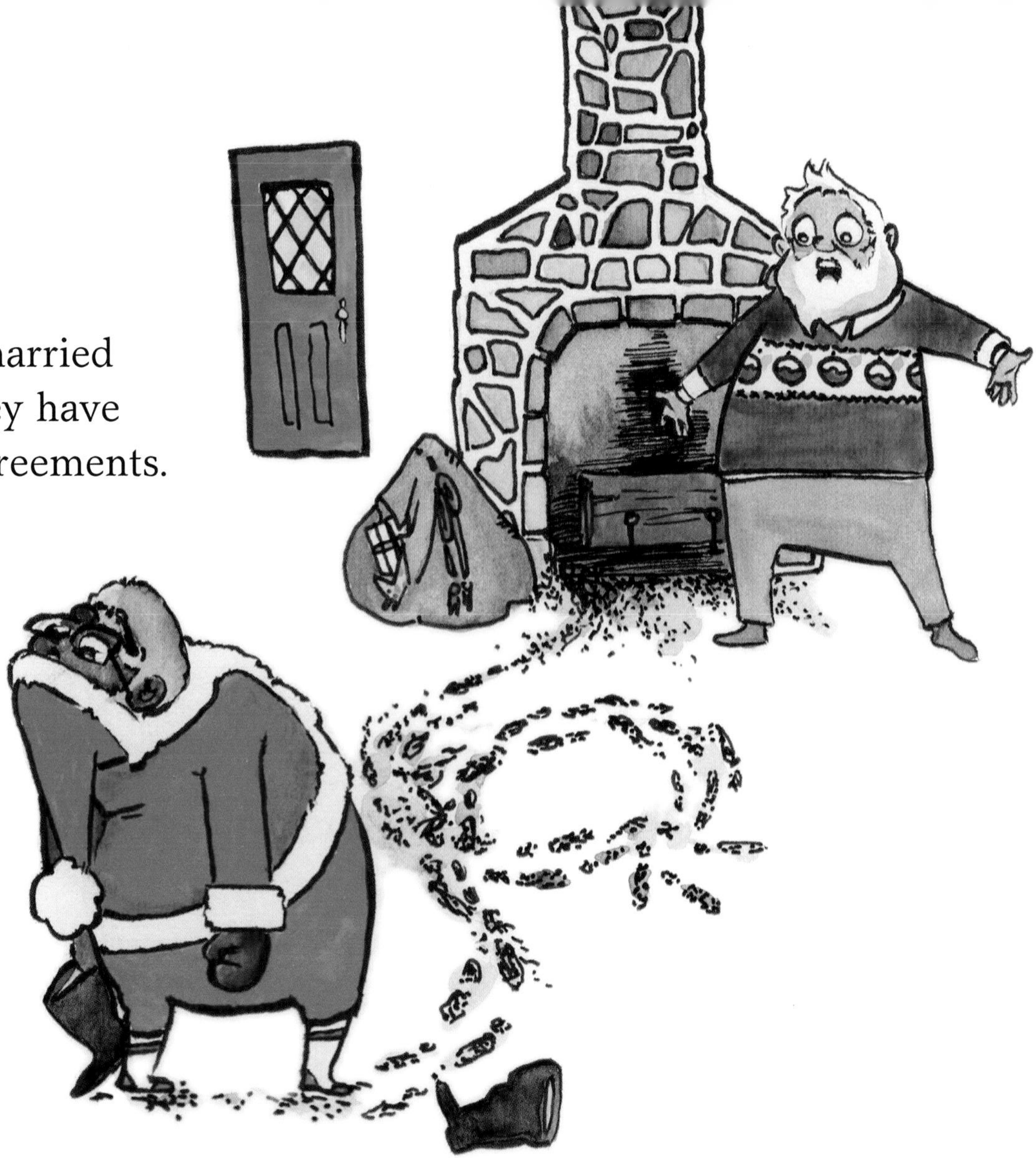

But they always manage to kiss and make up—
usually over a plate of milk and cookies.

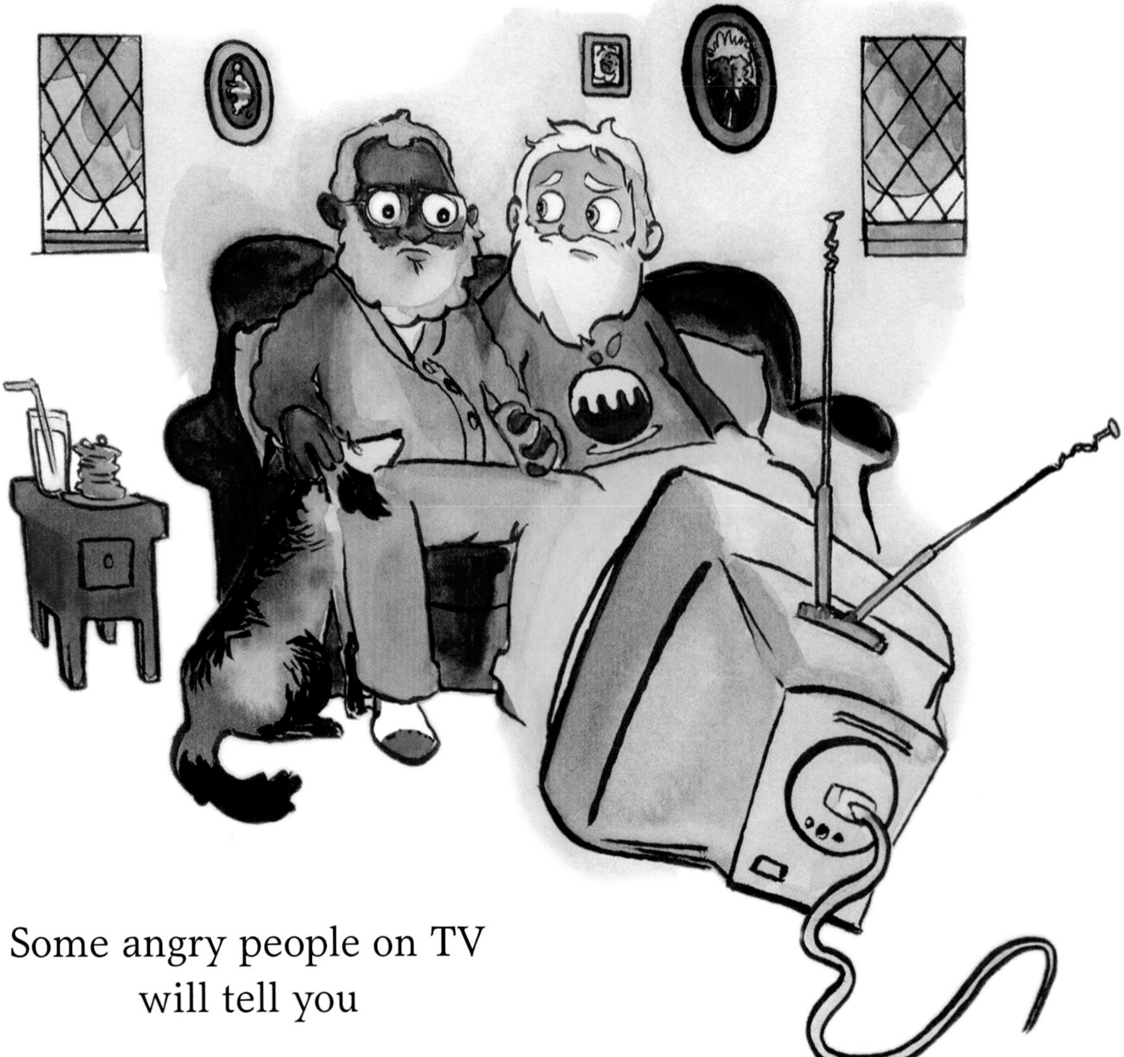

Some angry people on TV
will tell you

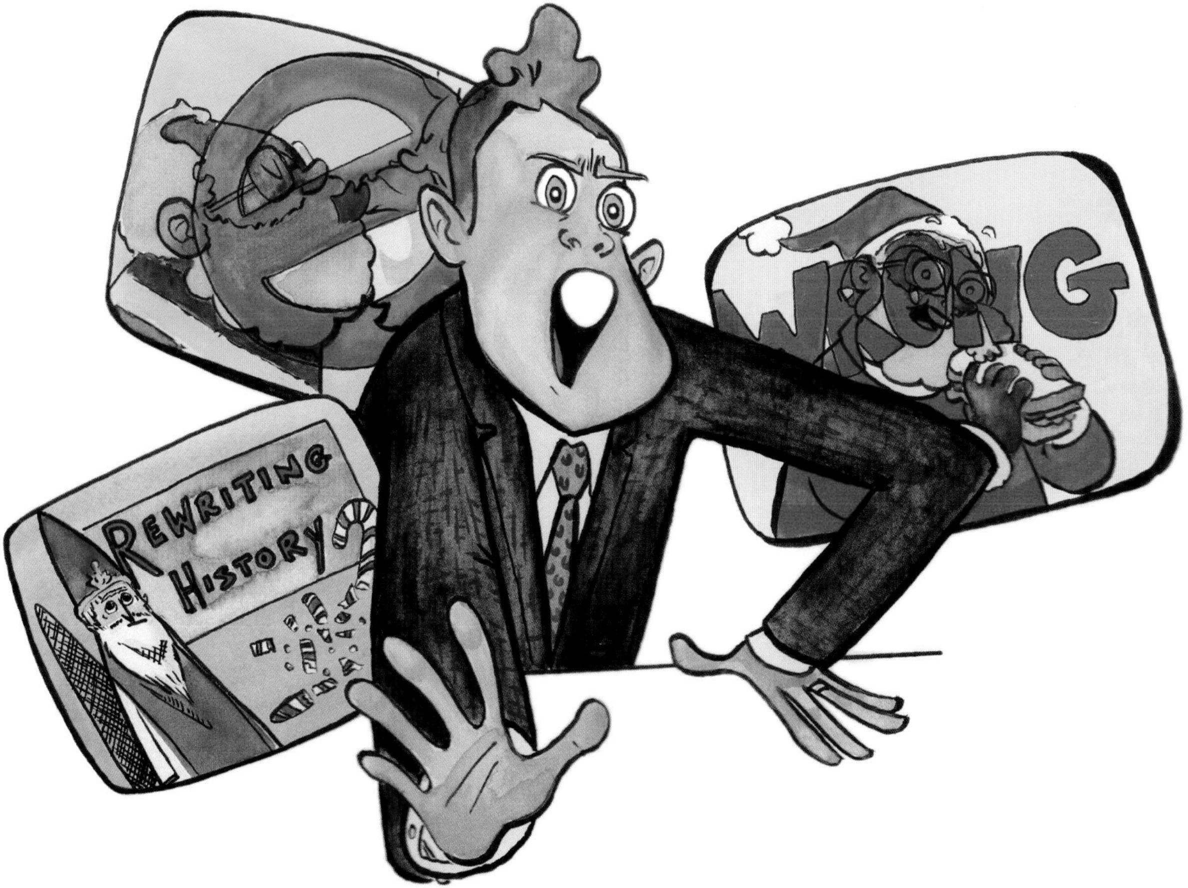
REWRITING HISTORY
WRONG

that this isn't what Santa Claus looks like—
or that Santa Claus doesn't even have a husband!

But people have
imagined Santa Claus
hundreds of different
ways over the years!

Who is anyone
to say what the real
Santa looks like?

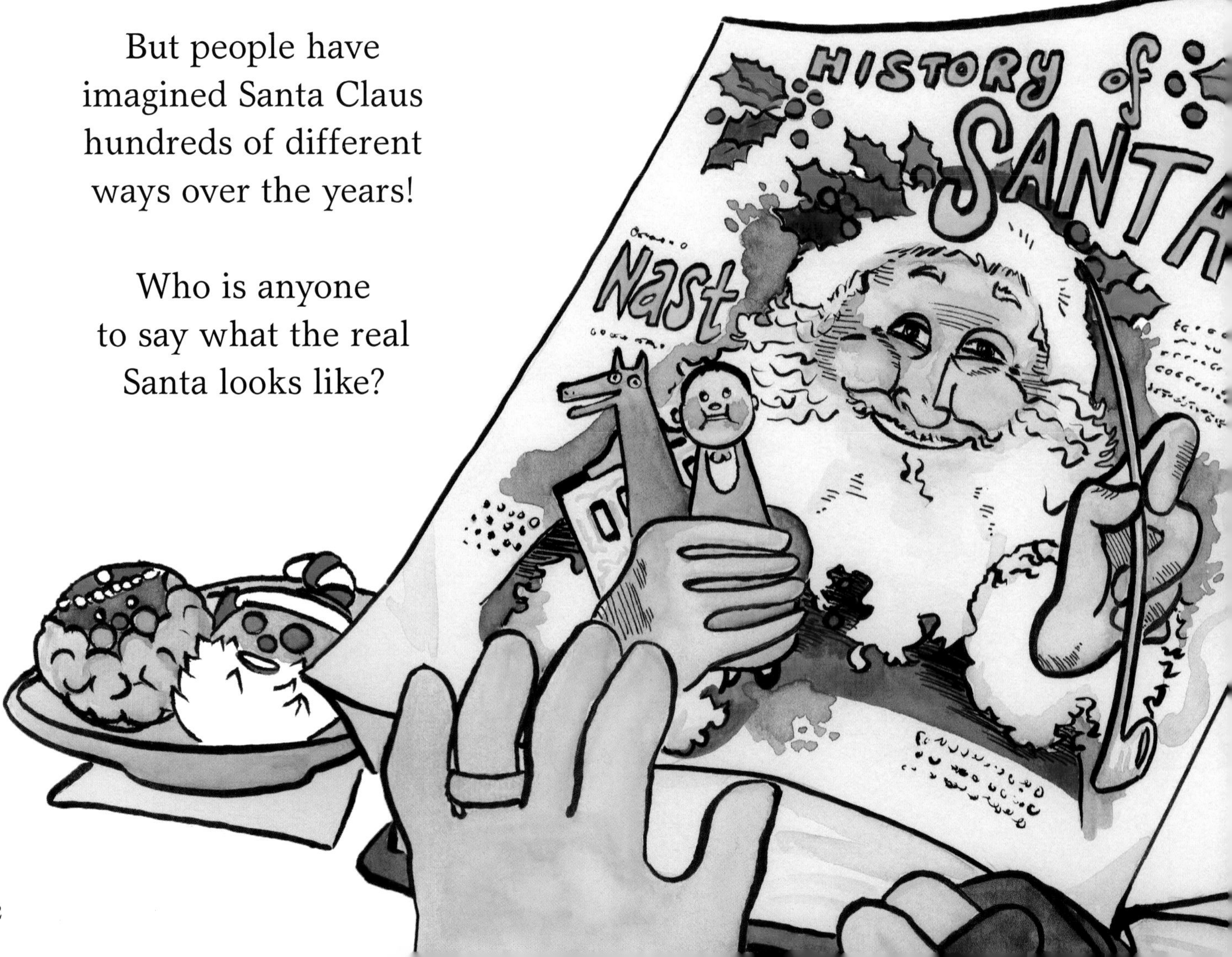
HISTORY of SANTA
Nast

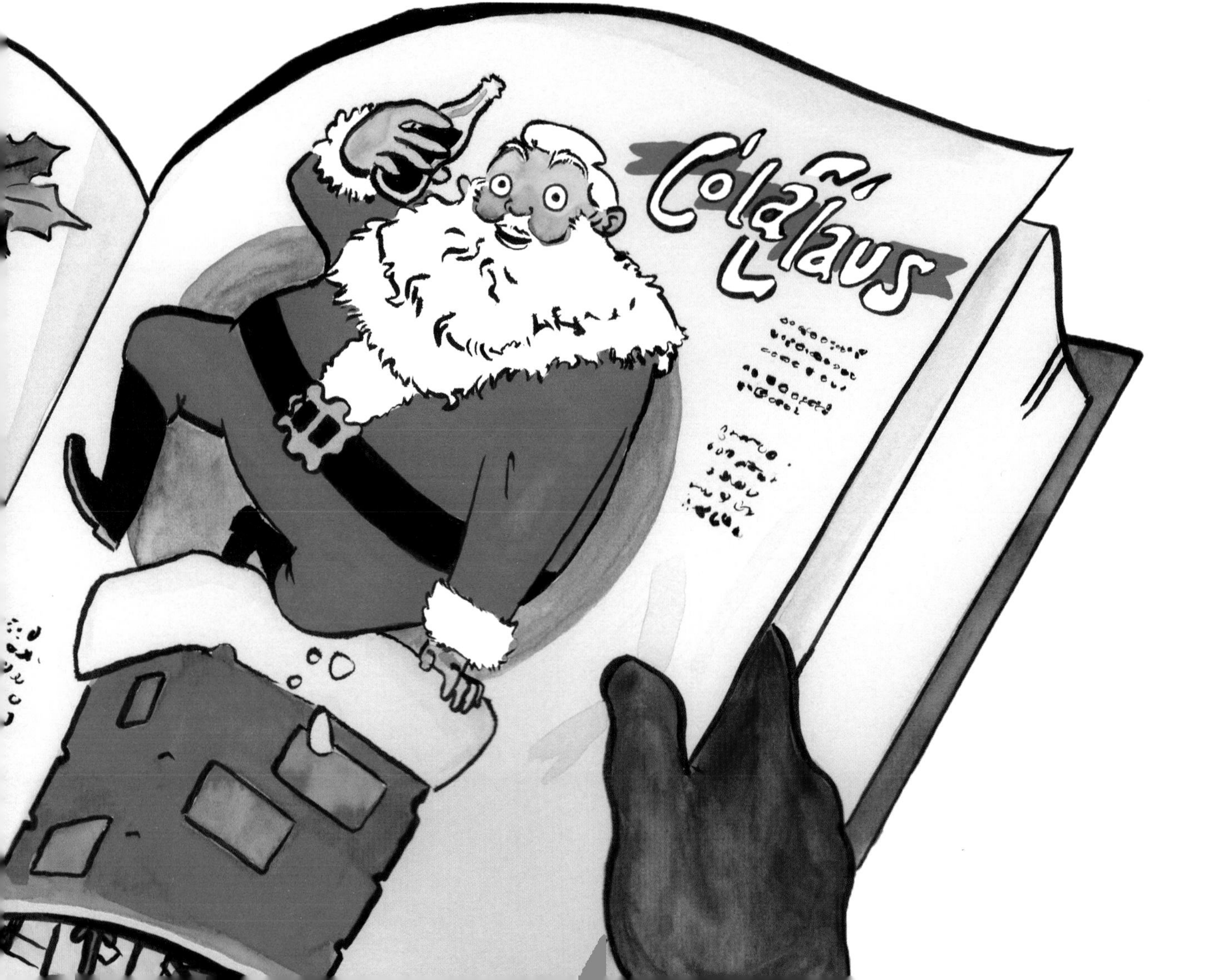

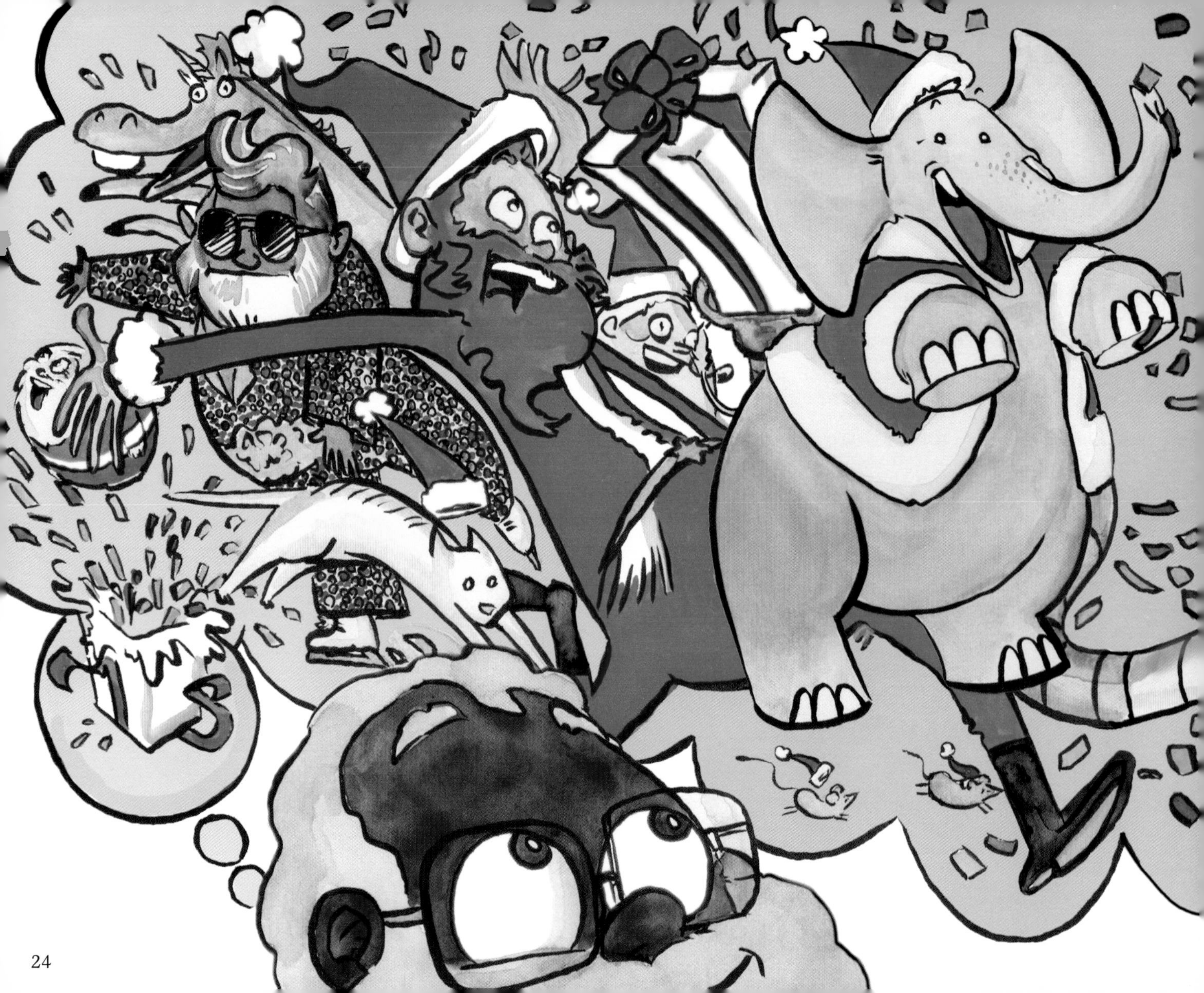

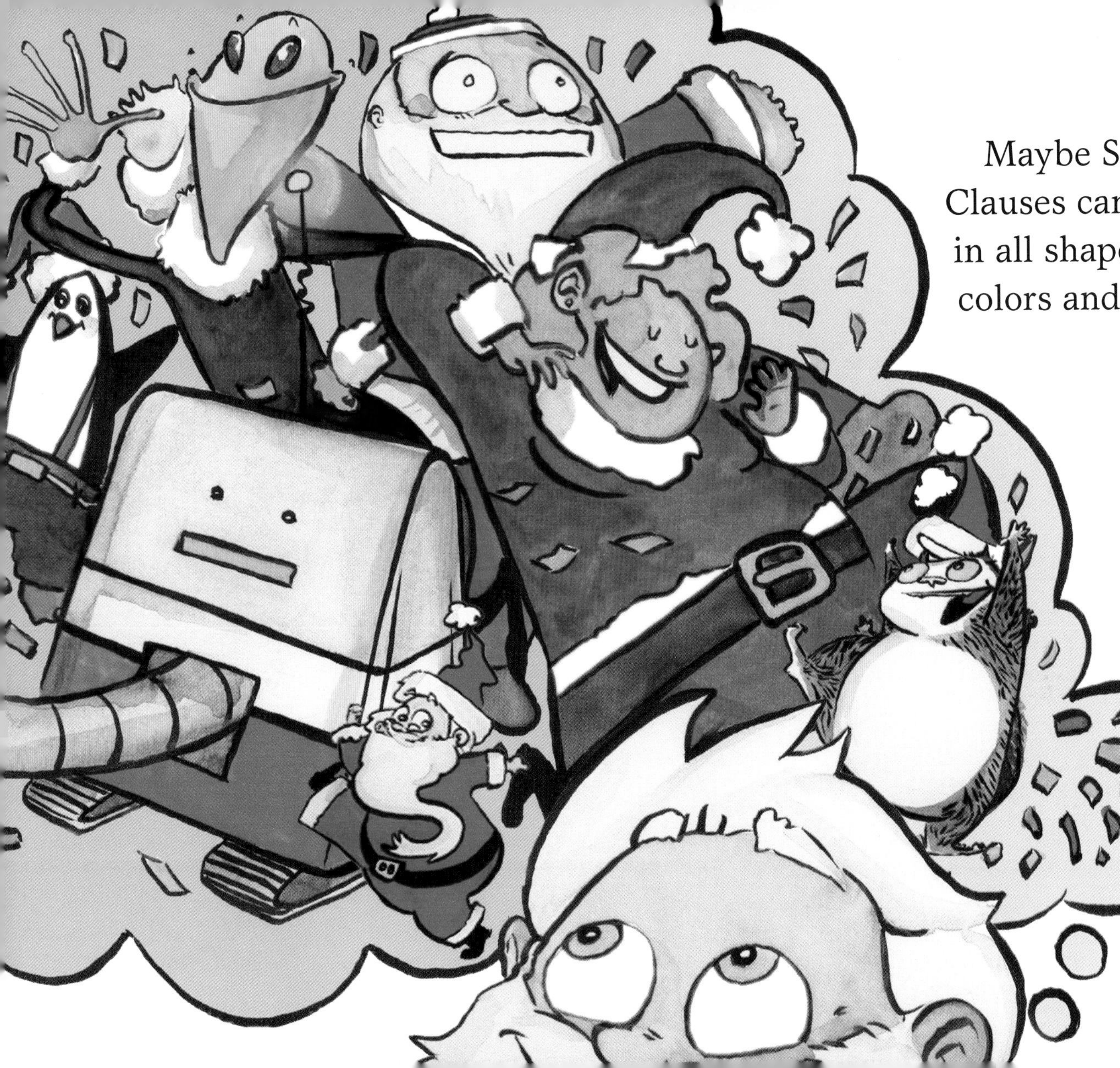

Maybe Santa Clauses can come in all shapes and colors and sizes!

Just like the
families that
Santa Claus
visits all over
the world.

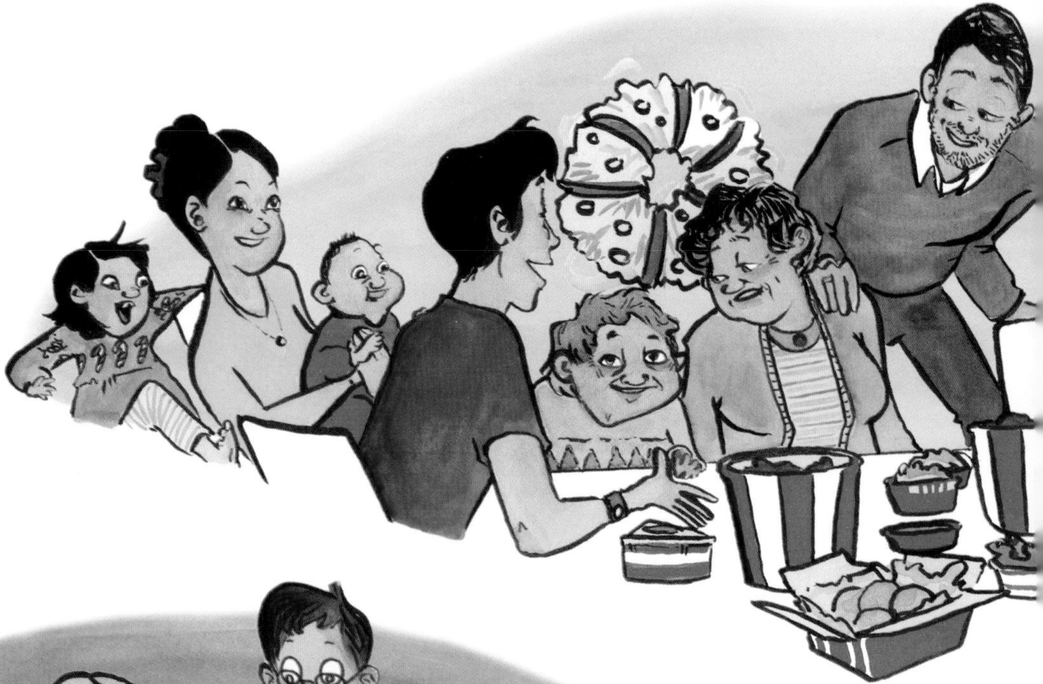

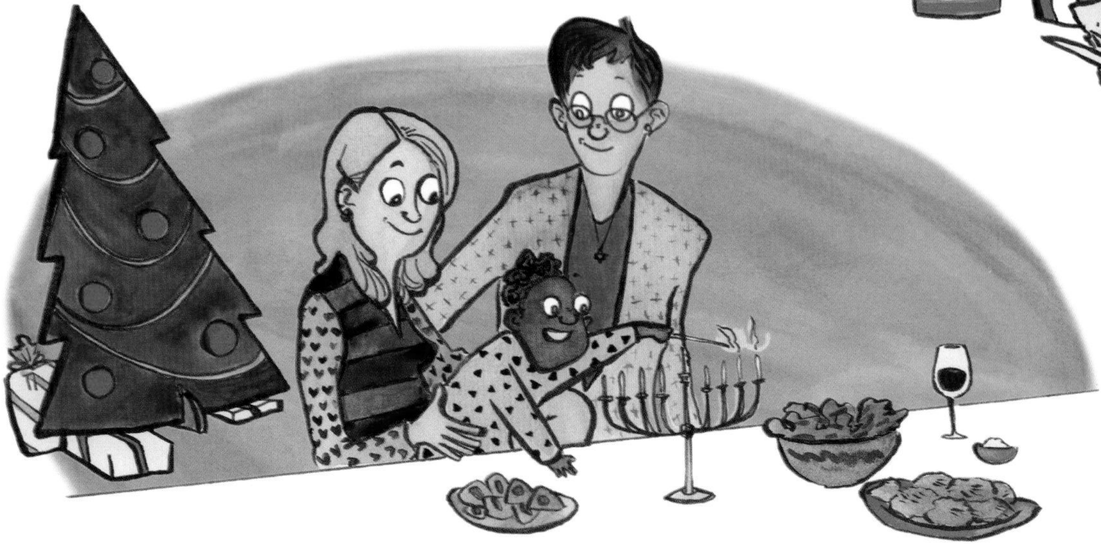

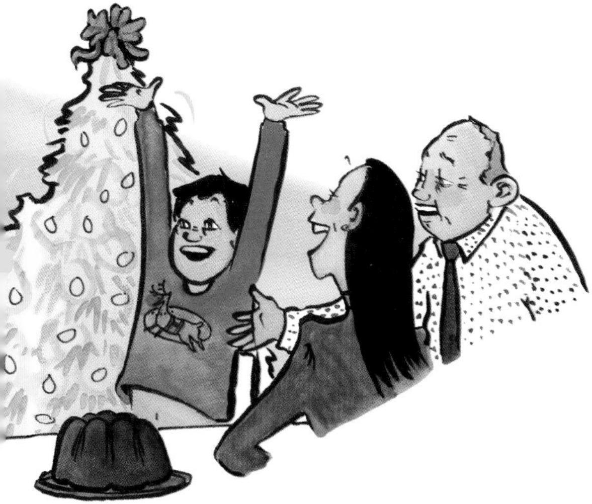

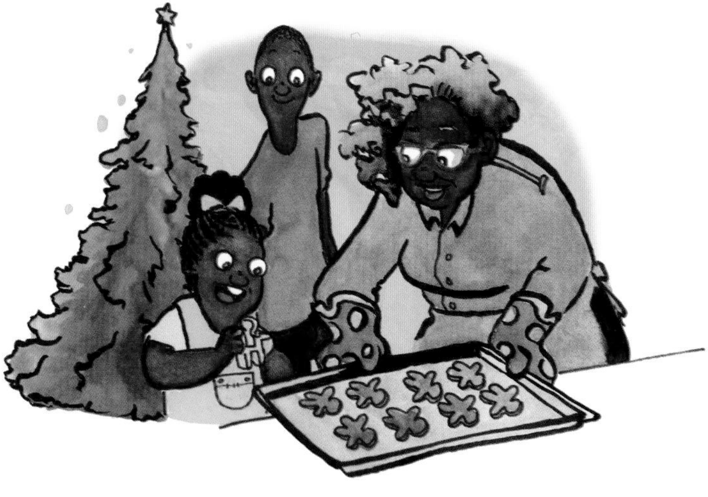

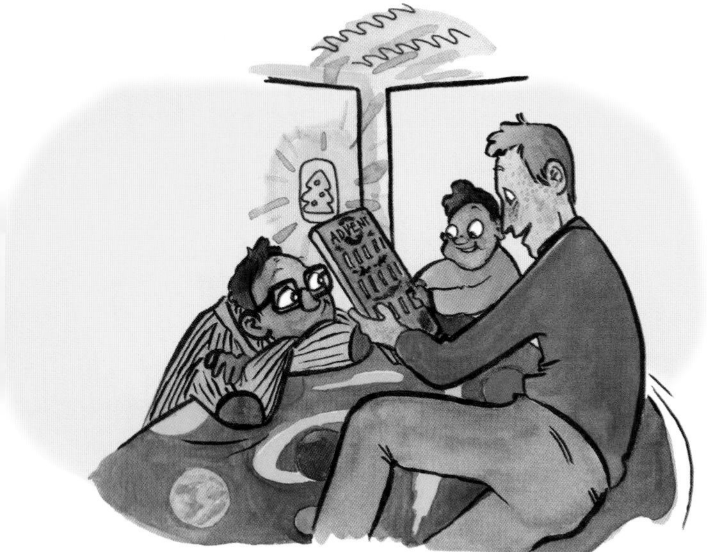
ADVENT

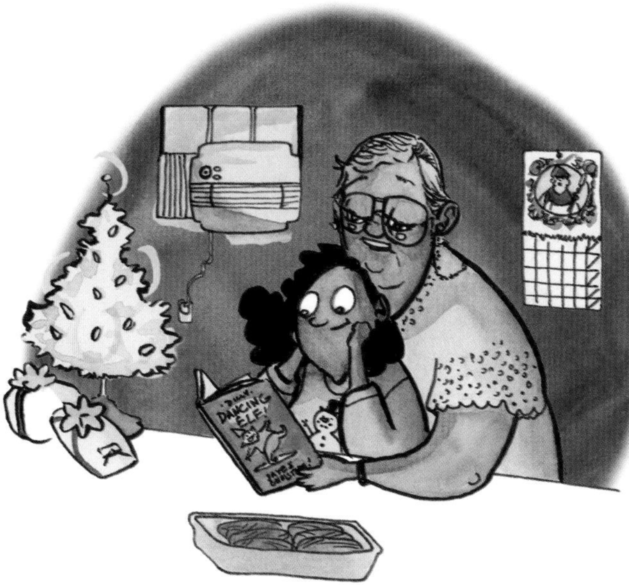
DANCING ELF!

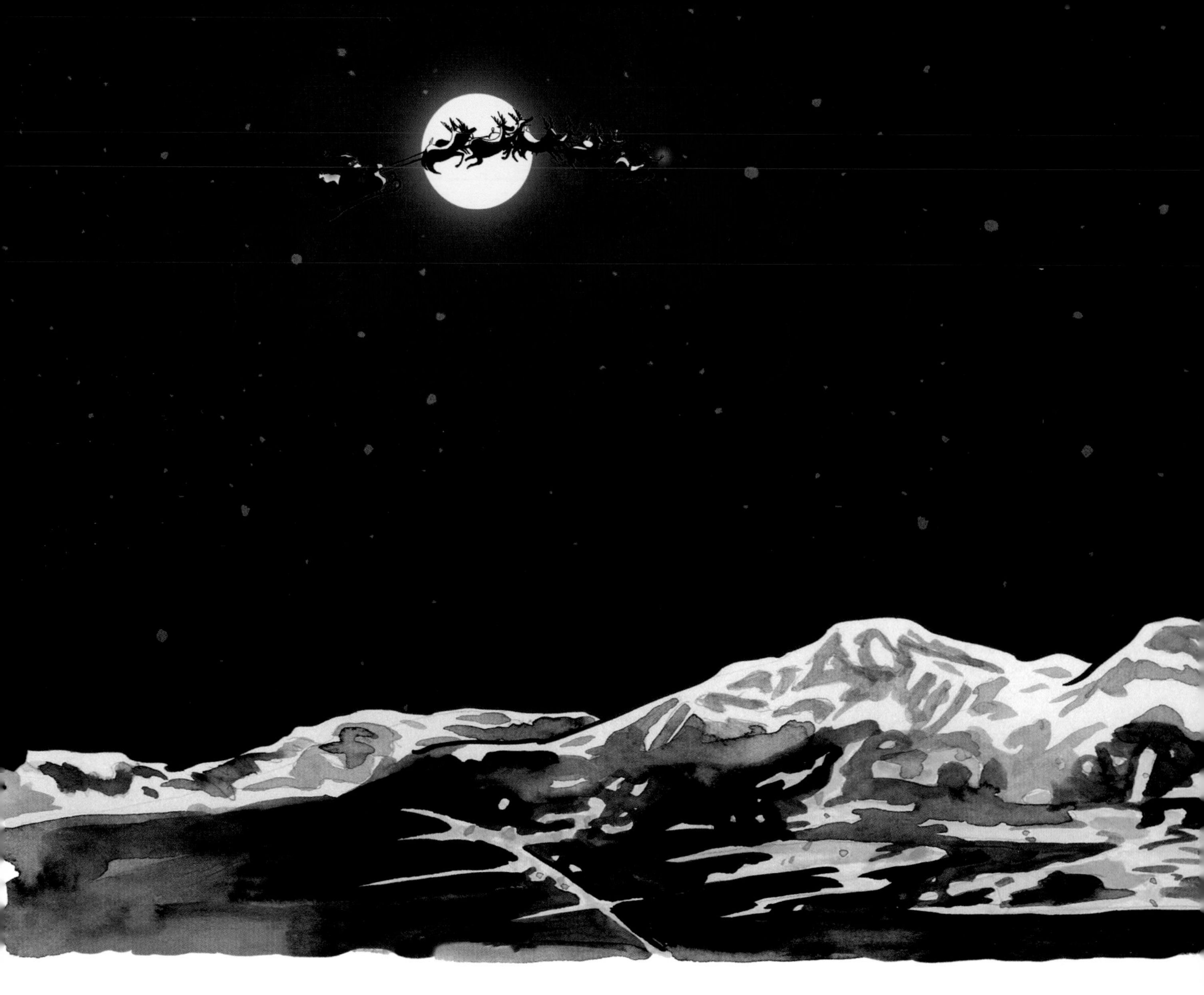

But as long as children believe
in the magic of Christmas, there will
always be a Santa Claus.

And as long as there is a Santa Claus, he will have a man waiting at home who loves him.

Also, Santa's husband's name is David.

About the Author and Illustrator

DANIEL KIBBLESMITH is a writer from Oak Park, Illinois. He is a staff writer for *The Late Show with Stephen Colbert* and a founding editor of *ClickHole*. He has written comics for Heavy Metal and Valiant Comics, comedy for *The New Yorker*, *McSweeney's*, *Onion News Network*, and *Funny or Die*, and is the co-author of the humor book *How to Win at Everything*. He works and lives in New York City.

ASHLEY QUACH is an illustrator in Los Angeles who lives in a house that's almost a hundred years old. She started drawing comics to amuse her students when she was an art teacher. Since then, she's drawn hundreds of comics, including the Internet hit *Boys' Night* and the wordless spooky story *Weirdy*. She is ambidextrous and can draw upside down.